GIRLS SURVIVE

Girls Survive is published by Stone Arch Books, an imprint of Capstone.
1710 Roe Crest Drive
North Mankato, Minnesota 56003
www.capstonepub.com

Library of Congress Cataloging-in-Publication Data
Names: Rogers, Andrea L., author. | Forsyth, Matt, illustrator. Title: Mary and the Trail of Tears : a Cherokee removal survival story / by Andrea L. Rogers ; illustrated by Matt Forsyth. Other titles: Girls survive. Description: North Mankato, Minnesota : Stone Arch Books, a Capstone imprint, 2020. | Series: Girls survive | Audience: Ages 8-12. | Summary: It is June first and twelve-year-old Mary does not really understand what is happening: she does not understand the hatred and greed of the white men who are forcing her Cherokee family out of their home in New Echota, Georgia, capital of the Cherokee Nation, and trying to steal what few things they are allowed to take with them, she does not understand why a soldier killed her grandfather--and she certainly does not understand how she, her sister, and her mother, are going to survive the thousand mile trip to the lands west of the Mississippi. Identifiers: LCCN 2019048028 (print) | LCCN 2019048029 (ebook) | ISBN 9781496587145 (hardcover) | ISBN 9781496592163 (paperback) | ISBN 9781496587152 (adobe pdf) Subjects: LCSH: Trail of Tears, 1838-1839--Juvenile fiction. | Cherokee Indians--History--19th century--Juvenile fiction. | Indians of North America--Southern States--History--Juvenile fiction. | Survival--Juvenile fiction. | Georgia--History--19th century--Juvenile fiction. | Southern States--History--19th century--Juvenile fiction. | CYAC: Trail of Tears, 1838-1839--Fiction. | Cherokee Indians--Fiction. | Indians of North America--Southern States--Fiction. | Survival--Fiction. | Georgia--History--19th century--Fiction. | Southern States--History--19th century--Fiction. | LCGFT: Historical fiction. Classification: LCC PZ7.1.R645 Mar 2020 (print) | LCC PZ7.1.R645 (ebook) | DDC 813.6 [Fic]--dc23 LC record available at https://lccn.loc.gov/2019048028 LC ebook record available at https://lccn.loc.gov/2019048029

Image Credits
Capstone Press, (map) 107, (triangle pattern) design element; Shutterstock: Spalnic, (paper) design element throughout; Phillip Robbins 2018, 112

Designers: Cynthia Della-Rovere and Charmaine Whitman
Cover Artist: Alessia Trunfio

Printed and bound in the United States of America.
3733

MARY AND THE TRAIL OF TEARS

A Cherokee Removal Survival Story

by Andrea L. Rogers

illustrated by Matt Forsyth

STONE ARCH BOOKS
a capstone imprint

CHAPTER ONE

Near New Echota, Georgia, capital of the Cherokee Nation
May 31, 1838
Late afternoon

The weather was hot and dry. Too hot to cook or work inside.

"Mary, no crop is more important to the Cherokees than corn," my older sister Margaret said. She was in charge of cooking dinner. She stirred dried corn and meat in an iron pot over the fire.

Margaret was only a few years older than me, but she talked like she thought she was an elder.

My grandma actually was an elder. She sat near us beading. For months she had been working on a beautiful bandolier bag. In the shade of a large oak, we all worked at different tasks.

I had a burden basket to finish. I was making a small one from splints of white oak. If all went well, it would fit me or my little sister, Becky.

Farther from the house, Mama and Becky worked in the garden. The corn was as tall as little Becky. She disappeared between the rows. She picked bugs off the stalks and fed them to her pet duck, Kawonu. Even though her duck could walk, Becky carried him everywhere. Kawonu didn't mind.

I wiped the sweat off my forehead with my sleeve. The shade from the tree helped a little. I was glad I didn't have to cook.

I hadn't worked on my basket in a while. I had soaked it in water to make it flexible. Now, as I pulled and pushed on the wooden splints, my fingers grew tender.

"Mary, do you think those sides are curved enough?" Margaret asked.

I frowned. I didn't want to remove its top

rows, so I stretched the sides out a bit. Instead of answering Margaret's question, I tried to change the subject. I wanted to be done with that basket. "Do you think we'll have to move west of the Mississippi?" I asked. "That's over a thousand miles away."

Margaret took longer to answer than I expected. Finally, she said, "Well, something has to change. We Cherokees have no rights in the state of Georgia. White men come in and steal, and we can't speak against them in court. Now the state of Georgia wants to divide our land into sections for white citizens, many of them want more land than they need."

"But it's illegal for a Cherokee to sell land! It says so in our constitution," I said. The Cherokee Constitution said that the land belonged to all of the Cherokee people. Taking more than you needed to live on was considered greedy.

Margaret nodded. "The penalty is death."

I had never heard Margaret talk like this. It frightened me. I turned to ask Grandma what she thought.

She had been sewing colorful glass beads into spirals and flowers on dark blue wool cloth earlier. Now, her hands were still, and her eyes were closed. She didn't look her usual energetic self. I got up, happy to put my basket down. I rubbed my sore fingers together.

"Grandma, can I get you anything?" I asked.

Grandma opened her eyes and nodded. "Can you bring me some cool water from the spring?" she replied.

I nodded. The spring-fed creek was just behind the cabin I lived in with my parents and sisters.

Over the years, the Cherokee community had helped my family build three log homes near one another. When everyone works together, it is called *gadugi*. We participated in gadugi when we helped other families too. Older people could count on the gadugi to help them with their personal gardens. In the summer, we would help harvest the corn in the larger fields. The labor of many people made hard tasks easier.

Nelly, my oldest sister, lived in the newest cabin. Two years ago, she had married Raven. He was a young Cherokee man who wore his hair long and neatly braided. Nelly was going to have her first baby this year. I smiled, thinking about the baby that was coming in the fall.

At the creek, I filled a bucket with cold, clear water. Even when there was very little rain, the creek was full. I gathered water for myself with a dipper gourd and drank mightily.

"Got a drink for an old man?" Grandpa called as he came out of the woods, holding several rabbits he had hunted.

I filled the gourd and leaped over the creek, then handed him the gourd.

Grandpa took a big drink. “Nothing tastes better than the water here, don’t you think?”

“Definitely, Grandpa.”

“Your daddy and Raven back yet?” he asked.

“No.”

“I hear New Echota is full of troops and almost empty of Cherokees,” Grandpa said.

Until a few years ago, New Echota had been our capital. It had housed a newspaper, the Cherokee Supreme Court, the Council house, a school, stores, and houses laid out in a grid system. Margaret often told me, “It’s the center of our nation. Like Athens was for the Greeks.”

“Jenny and her family left New Echota a while back. Before General Scott got to Fort Wool,” I said.

Jenny was Raven’s niece, the daughter of his sister, Charlotte. She was also my best friend.

I hadn't seen much of her since the soldiers invaded our land, and I missed her and her little brother, Steven.

Grandpa thought for a minute. "Yes, Raven said his sister had gone back to their mother's home. I never thought I'd live to see so much cruelty. New roads, forts, and stockades built all over Cherokee land," he said as he stared past me.

I looked around too. I saw our cabins and the land in a way I hadn't before. Behind me were the woods. How many times had I gone there with Grandma to gather plants? The creator provided food and medicine we couldn't grow in the garden. The woods were home to the deer and bears and rabbits we hunted. Mom's brother, Uncle Rock, had taken me and my sisters to hunt there before he and his wife had moved west.

Mama's family had lived on this land for a long time. Our kin were buried near the woods behind our home. Relatives gone long before I was born lay next to children who hadn't lived long enough for me to get to know as my brothers and sisters and cousins.

As Grandpa walked toward the house, I remembered what I wanted to tell him. "I don't think Grandma is feeling well. She asked me to get her some water."

"Well, it's hot," Grandpa said, nodding. He handed me the rabbits. "Take these to the smokehouse." He picked up the water bucket and walked toward Grandma as I went to the smokehouse.

Grandma and Grandpa were gone by the time I got back to the shade of the oak tree. I sat down and picked up my basket, determined to finish it. I pulled out the top rows and started again. This time, I paid close attention to the shape. The bottom was the right square shape, and I worked slowly so the top curved out gracefully, like a bowl.

I glanced up at Margaret, who was watching me

with a smile. I folded down the tops of the basket and folded the weavers back inside to give the top a nice, clean edge.

Margaret was about to speak when we heard Becky squeal in a happy voice, "Daddy!"

Daddy and Raven were coming back on their horses. They were visible farther down the road. "Go see if Nelly's awake. Tell her it's time to eat," Margaret said.

I ran to the cabin Raven and Nelly shared and knocked on the door. Nelly opened it immediately. Instead of napping, she had been working at her weaving loom. Next to the loom was a basket of yarn that Margaret had spun over the winter.

"You're going to have more blankets than that baby will need in a lifetime," I said.

Nelly laughed. "Couldn't sleep. Finished another." She gestured to the blue and white cloth. She would trade, sell, or give away the extra.

"You make these faster than I can make a basket," I groaned. "I did finally finish the one I've been working on, though."

"You'll get the hang of basketmaking. If you want to," Nelly said.

As I followed her into the yard, I wasn't sure if that was true.

Daddy was in the garden speaking to Mama. He looked tired and unhappy. After a few minutes, they stopped talking. Mama crossed her arms. Her mouth was turned down in a frown. She knelt at the bed of collard greens and pulled enough for supper. Then she and Daddy walked toward the cabin, no longer speaking.

"I wonder what Daddy found out," I whispered to Nelly, my insides knotted with worry.

"I don't know if I want to know," Nelly replied, just as quietly.

CHAPTER TWO

Near New Echota
May 31, 1838
Evening, almost sundown

Mama passed me on her way into our cabin. "Mary, heat up the grease to make the greens," she said.

One of my favorite things to eat was wilted greens. I fetched a pot full of bacon grease and a small iron skillet. I scooped the soft grease into the pan and returned the pot to the pantry shelf. Back at the fire, I heated up the grease so it got just hot enough to melt but not burn. By the time I went inside, my family was seated at the table. The adults talked quietly. Grandma didn't look well at all.

I poured the hot grease over the greens and sat down at Grandma's side.

Since our cabin was the largest, we ate most of our evening meals there together. Like the other cabins, it had a fireplace and wood floors. My sisters and I slept in the loft, and my parents slept below us in the back of the cabin.

"The Georgians took sixteen Cherokees to Fort Wool," Daddy said. "They told the general they wanted them whipped."

"What had they done, Daddy?" I cried.

"It's a crime to be Cherokee," Raven said quietly.

"Did they whip them?" Becky asked.

"General Scott didn't allow it. But he is moving quickly on removing us," Daddy said. "Thousands of troops are coming to force us out. There are prison camps built all over Cherokee Nation." He paused for a moment. "Scott told Assistant Chief George Lowery that he could not be held responsible for the treatment of our people if we resist."

Daddy quoted Davy Crockett. "Happy days of Republican principles are near at an end when a few is to transfer the many."

"What does that mean?" I asked.

"Well, a few Cherokees illegally signed a treaty for a whole nation. If the will of the majority can be defeated by a few men, the United States is in trouble." He paused. "Maybe those treaty signers thought that, no matter what, the Cherokees' land would be taken. Most of our nation disagrees with them. The United States Supreme Court agreed with us, yet Congress accepted the illegal treaty."

Everyone was silent.

I was frightened. *Are the soldiers on their way now?* I wondered.

Grandma reached over and held my hand. Her hands were cold and damp.

"Well, we can't do anything about it tonight," Mama said. "Might as well eat before the food gets cold."

The evening sun streamed in through our cabin door, lighting the table as we ate. After dinner, Margaret and Becky stayed at the table. Becky was learning to write the Cherokee syllabary.

She handled an old copy of the Cherokee newspaper called the *Cherokee Phoenix*. The paper had closed down about four years earlier when the nation could no longer afford to print it, but we kept a stack of old issues.

"I bet the governor hated that this paper was printed in both English and Cherokee," I said, looking at the different columns.

"Most Georgians hated the paper for that reason and more," Margaret said. "It let the world know about the terrible things going on here." Her voice shook with emotion as she sorted through the old newspapers. "Words can destroy nations. But they can build nations too. Our Constitution was one of the first things printed on that press. It's right here." She held out a paper in front of us and pointed at a column.

Becky and I looked over at the old newspaper.

"That's the Constitution?" Becky asked.

"Yes," said Margaret. "It's here on the front page of the *Cherokee Phoenix*'s first issue."

From the other side of the room, the sound of a violin could be heard. Grandpa had a fiddle that had belonged to his own grandfather. He played a sweet tune Grandma liked. Outside, it was getting dark. Fireflies drifted up out of the grass. Tree frogs sang.

Grandpa began to play something low. It sounded sad.

"What's that song called?" Becky asked.

"It's 'Orphan Child,'" Margaret said.

"Who is that song about?"

Grandma leaned over and spoke gently to Becky. "It's about us. It means the creator wants us to take care of each other. If a child is alone and crying, we need to take care of them."

Nelly and Raven got up to go. Before she left, Nelly hugged Grandma. Grandpa put away his fiddle. He and Daddy talked some more. Grandma and Mama walked out to the garden to put up the chickens.

Margaret began to pick up the dishes. "Can you and Becky tighten the bed?" Margaret asked me.

Margaret, Becky, and I shared a bed in the loft. Becky slept in the middle. Lately, Margaret and I had been rolling into the middle too. The ropes that held the mattress had stretched, making the bed sag.

Becky and I climbed the ladder to the loft.

I fetched the rope wrench to tighten the ropes. We removed the feather-filled mattress and passed the wrench back and forth. Becky and I worked until the weave was tight again. We lifted the mattress back onto the bed.

I shook out the blankets. Becky's cornhusk doll was in the middle of them. I put the doll in my apron pocket. I planned to go back downstairs and put in on the table. Becky would want to play with it in the morning.

Becky climbed into bed. Her eyelids were heavy.

"Goodnight, Possum," I said.

"You and Margaret aren't going to squish me tonight?" she asked. She wrinkled her nose at me.

I held up the wrench. "We're going to sleep tight tonight."

Becky smiled and rolled onto her side.

I went downstairs to help Margaret clean up. As I stepped off the ladder, I heard Mama shout from the garden. Grandpa and Daddy dashed outside.

"Do you think it's the soldiers?" I whispered to Margaret.

But Margaret ran outside without answering. I watched cautiously from the porch. In the low light, I saw Raven and Daddy carry Grandma to her cabin. Frightened, I ran across the grass to my grandparents' small cabin.

CHAPTER THREE

Mary's grandparents' cabin, Near New Echota
May 31, 1838
Late night

Nelly had followed Raven to Grandma's cabin too. "What happened?" I whispered to her.

"Mama said Grandma touched her chest and fell in the garden," she answered.

From the doorway of my grandparents' bedroom, I saw that Grandma wasn't answering Grandpa or Mama.

Margaret moved around the cabin, getting the things Mama requested. I tried to stay out of the way. I didn't know what to do to help. I followed Margaret to the cupboard and asked if she wanted me to go back home and get medicine. We had gathered different plants with Grandma over the years. Surely there was something that would help.

Margaret had already taken some dried leaves from the cabinet. “Bring me some hot water,” she said. “I’ll make tea.”

I did as I was told, trying to stay busy. Nelly walked with me to heat up water over the still-burning fire before she returned to her own home.

As quickly as I could, I returned with the iron teapot. After Margaret made tea, she gave it to Mama.

“Go on home, girls,” Mama said. “I’ll stay here.”

Margaret and I went back to our cabin and got into bed. Between us, Becky slept peacefully. I had trouble falling asleep.

Before long, Daddy returned. I heard him getting ready for bed. I tried to stay awake, but fell asleep before I heard Mama come back home.

When I woke up the next morning, I felt like I had barely closed my eyes. I rolled toward my sisters. Margaret was no longer in bed. I heard someone cooking downstairs.

I was tired, but I didn't wait to be asked to help this time. I got up and got dressed.

"Mama?" I said, as I came down the ladder.

"Your grandma died last night," Mama replied.

I felt like crying. My grandma was gone. Who would teach me to bead? Who would take me to the woods and patiently tell me the uses of the many plants? There was so much I hadn't learned. Grandma had stayed with us while Mama worked the fields. She fed us and doctored us. Now she would be buried with her ancestors in the burial yard.

"Your father went to the neighbor's house to make the coffin," Mama said. "Margaret is taking care of things at your grandparents' place."

At my grandparents' home, Margaret would spend

the morning getting Grandma's body dressed and ready for burial. The funeral would be the next day. Until then, someone would need to sit with the body.

I went to let the chickens out. Watching them usually made me feel better when I was sad. I didn't have much time to watch them that morning, though. I gathered eggs and ran them back to the cabin for breakfast. In the yard, I gathered green onions and took those back to Mama too. When Mama finished cooking breakfast, she put some food on a plate. "Here," she said. "Take this to Raven and Nelly. Go eat with them. I'm not hungry."

I hugged her. "You should go rest." I was sure she had been up all night.

"I might."

The door of Nelly's cabin was open. Raven and Nelly sat at a little table. Their cabin was a smaller version of ours.

"Daddy's gone," I said, handing the food to Nelly.

Raven nodded. "I know. I'm going to go dig the grave."

Nelly dished the food onto plates. We ate quietly.

Afterward, Nelly got a large woven cloth from her trunk. "You take this over to Margaret," she said.

I knew the cloth would be wrapped around Grandma for her burial. As Raven got ready to leave, I took the fabric to Margaret in my grandparents' cabin. She seemed tired. When I came home, I found Mama asleep. Becky called to me from the loft.

"I'll bring you some food, Becky," I replied.

I reached into my apron pocket and found Becky's cornhusk doll. I put cold cornbread, eggs, and onions on a plate. I balanced it carefully and climbed the ladder. Becky ate. We played quietly with the cornhusk doll while Mama slept. I told Becky that Grandma had died, and she cried for a little bit.

Time passed slowly. I got a strip of cloth to wrap around the basket I had made. Becky filled its bottom with dry grass and set Kawonu in it. I tied it around Becky's shoulders. She carried the duck all over. We ended up behind the cabin playing in the creek.

We waved at Raven when he looked up from his shovel. He waved back.

Suddenly the sound of a wagon and horses caught our attention. From where we stood, we could see the road. To our surprise, the men coming down the road were white men. A few were dressed as soldiers, in matching pants and hats, and carrying musket rifles. Men in a second wagon were also holding rifles, but they weren't in uniform.

"Run to the cabin!" Raven said.

Raven was faster than us. He picked up Becky and ran, dragging me along behind them. When we reached the cabin, he set Becky down and let go of my hand. Mama ran out of the cabin and grabbed Becky. Raven kept running, shouting that soldiers were coming.

CHAPTER FOUR

Near New Echota
June 1, 1838
Afternoon

When we ran into the cabin, Mama slammed the door behind us. I helped her slide the wooden plank that barred the door shut into place.

"Go upstairs, Becky," Mama ordered.

Becky scooted up the loft ladder.

I heard the other cabins' doors slam shut. Peeking through a crack in the logs, I watched a wagon pull into the yard and stop right in front of our cabin. My heart pounded in my ears. I couldn't tell what the men were shouting. Two men in uniforms climbed down and approached our home.

The other wagon pulled up next to the stable where the livestock were kept. Our two horses weren't in there, though. Daddy had needed them to pull the wagon when he went to the neighbors.

All the men in the yard carried guns. Several rifles had pointed bayonets.

"It's the federal soldiers," Mama said softly.

"Who are the other men?" I whispered.

"People who want our things," Mama said through clenched teeth. "Georgia militia, maybe."

The sharp smack of the butt of a rifle hit the door next to our heads. I jumped away, frightened. My heart beat louder than the man pounding on the door.

"Go up to the loft," Mama said. I didn't want to leave her, but I did as I was told.

One man was yelling through the door in English. Margaret spoke and understood English better than anyone else in the family, but she was in the other cabin with Grandpa.

A second voice spoke through the door. I recognized it as Mr. McFarland. He was a white man my Uncle Rock had given work to once years ago. Recently though, Mr. McFarland had moved his family into another Cherokee's property and kicked the Cherokee family out. It made me mad that it was him at our door, yelling at us in Cherokee.

"You all have to go now!" Mr. McFarland hollered. "The President has been patient long enough. This ain't your home no more."

The soldier who spoke only English appeared to be in charge. He seemed to be telling Mr. McFarland what to say in Cherokee.

"Lieutenant Smith says come out now," Mr. McFarland said.

Suddenly we heard Margaret's voice outside. I rushed back down the ladder. Mama looked terrified. I felt as afraid as she looked. She started to slide the plank back to open the door. I reached out and stopped her.

"Wait, Mama," I whispered.

I knew Margaret was explaining to him in English that there had been a death in the family, that we needed to have a funeral the next day. I was glad she could speak for us. I didn't trust that interpreter.

The lieutenant responded, but I didn't understand what he said.

Meanwhile, Mama had started grabbing things. She hurriedly dropped them into a large burden basket. She grabbed a blanket off her bed and stuffed it in. On top of that, she put a pot. She grabbed the flint pieces from where they sat on the pantry shelf and stuck them in her pocket.

"Go get some more clothes on. Have Becky do it too," she said frantically. "And get some of Margaret's clothes. And all the moccasins."

I ran back up the loft ladder and started grabbing

clothes. “Put your moccasins on, Becky,” I said. I shoved a dress at her. “Here, put this on over your clothes.”

“But Mary, it’s hot!” Becky argued.

“Can’t be helped, Becky.” I leaned down and kissed her cheek. “I’m sorry, Possum.”

I helped her slip the dress on over the one she was wearing. I was glad Kawonu was already asleep in the basket. It would be one less thing to try to grab. I slipped a blanket in under the sleeping duck. It quacked angrily. I grabbed Margaret’s moccasins and threw them into the basket too.

Outside, the white men were taking our livestock. The chickens were screeching and crying, trying to run away. I felt helpless and angry.

“Mama!” Margaret’s shaky voice called through the door. “Open the door, Mama.”

Mama went to the door and pulled the wooden plank back.

"Mama, I'm sorry." Margaret was crying angry tears.

Mama shook her head. She handed Margaret the basket and asked her to help her tie it onto her back.

Mr. McFarland spoke up, "Y'all don't need to take anything. The government's going to give you everything you need for your trip. Now come on out." He reached for the basket Margaret was holding.

The other soldier snapped at him, and Mr. McFarland took his greedy hands away.

I grabbed the small burden basket. If the men tried to take the basket from Becky, she might get hurt trying to save her pet duck.

I whispered to Becky. "Let me carry it for you. But don't say anything about it. If those men think it's valuable, they will take it," I warned. Becky helped me tie it to my back.

I heard the lieutenant ask Margaret something while he looked at a paper.

Margaret gestured toward the neighbors' place. The soldier frowned. Across the yard, there was more shouting. Several men stood with guns pointed at Nelly's door. Margaret and the lieutenant ran across the yard. Lieutenant Smith yelled at the Georgians. I hoped he was telling them not to shoot Nelly and Raven. When the door opened, the men rushed into Nelly's house.

"Y'all better not move," Mr. McFarland said to Becky, Mama, and me. He turned and disappeared inside our cabin. We could hear him opening drawers and moving things around.

More shouting came from Grandpa's cabin. A Georgian escorted Grandpa out, a rifle between Grandpa's shoulder blades. Grandpa walked stiffly out of the home he had raised his family in. He held an object wrapped in cloth close to his chest. The guard walked behind him until they arrived at the wagon in front of our home.

Mama walked cautiously to meet him. The man with the rifle turned away. He walked back to Grandma and Grandpa's cabin. We could hear things being thrown around. Chairs tipped over on the wooden floors. Lids lifted off pots.

Since gold had been discovered on Cherokee land a decade earlier, many Georgians were convinced we had gold hidden away. They didn't understand that to us the most valuable things were other Cherokees. Grandpa's own grandfather had taught him to play the violin that he now held wrapped in cloth in front of him. He set it gently into Mama's basket. As Grandpa reached me and Becky, he put his strong arms around both of us.

From every corner of our property, the men argued over my family's things. Georgians marched Raven out of his house with his hands tied in front of him. His hair was messy, and his cheek was swollen. The red cloth that tied his hair into a braid

was missing. Nelly walked behind him crying quietly. She held her arms across her belly. I felt sick.

The soldier in charge climbed up onto the wagon's seat. He turned to Margaret and said something to her. She turned to Grandpa and asked him if he wanted to ride in the wagon. He looked angrily at the soldier and shook his head.

"Where are we going?" I asked, trying to sound brave for Becky.

Margaret repeated my question in English.

"Fort Wool at New Echota," he said.

"Will Daddy be there?" I asked Margaret. She relayed my question.

He answered with a shrug.

I turned and looked back at our house as the wagon began to roll forward. As the lieutenant urged the horses on, Mama, Margaret, Nelly, Becky, Raven, Grandpa, and I began to walk. Grandpa dropped behind us. We didn't notice when he stopped walking. However, the lieutenant saw and stopped the wagon. Grandpa turned and ran back toward his house.

The lieutenant yelled. I knew he was telling Grandpa to stop. Grandpa kept running and disappeared into his cabin. He didn't want to leave my grandmother.

They had hit Raven and bound his hands. My grandpa was strong, but he was much older than Raven. I was afraid they were going to beat my grandpa or whip him when we got to the fort.

Grandpa was only in the house a moment when a single rifle shot exploded.

CHAPTER FIVE

Near New Echota
June 1, 1838
Evening

A white Georgian with a rifle walked out of my grandparents' home. The lieutenant jumped back down from the wagon and returned to the cabin, taking Margaret with him.

I held my breath, expecting Grandpa to be escorted out. I was sure his hands would be bound, like Raven's. Several minutes later, Margaret and Lieutenant Smith returned. Tears streamed down Margaret's face. The lieutenant looked mad. He climbed back up and urged the horses on.

"Mama?" I said.

Mama was crying loudly now. She didn't look back at me.

In the front of the wagon, the lieutenant was speaking angrily. *Is he going to shoot us?* I wondered.

I whispered to Margaret, "What is he saying?"

"He says, 'I told him he couldn't stay,'" Margaret said through tears.

"What happened, Margaret? Where is Grandpa?" I said urgently. "Is he hurt?"

Margaret swallowed before answering. "That soldier shot him. He killed him. The lieutenant asked him 'What for?' and that soldier said he wouldn't be happy until every Cherokee in Georgia was dead."

I felt shaky and afraid. We had heard about violent evictions. The Choctaws' and Creeks' homes and lands were sometimes set on fire to get them to leave. Now, my grandma had died, and my grandpa had been murdered. Neither of them would be laid to rest by our community. Their graves would be forgotten.

None of us said anything. Becky began to cry loudly. I, too, began to weep. Nelly also wailed.

Suddenly, when we had lost sight of the cabin, the lieutenant stopped the horses and climbed down from the wagon. We all froze.

He pulled out his knife and walked over to Raven.

"No!" Nelly screamed.

The soldier glanced at her before he grabbed Raven's arms and cut the rope that was binding his wrists.

The lieutenant pointed at Becky and then at Raven, "Put that little girl up here," Margaret said, translating for him. Raven lifted her up. "Put your baskets in there too."

Margaret helped Mama untie her basket and put it in the wagon. Raven set my basket into the wagon. Becky reached in and pulled out Kawonu. The duck ran around the back of the wagon, quacking quietly as the lieutenant climbed back onto the wagon's front seat. While Becky rode, the rest of us walked next to the wagon. Our light tan moccasins were quickly getting dusty.

The sun was going down as the wagon drew closer to New Echota, where Fort Wool had been established. I didn't recognize the town. The woods that once surrounded the town were flattened. In the distance, I saw the stockade that surrounded Fort Wool. Logs stood side by side, their tips sharpened.

I hoped Daddy would be there waiting. I felt exhausted. I wondered if there would be someplace comfortable to sleep.

The wagon pulled through the fort's gates. Mama was still weeping, staring off into the distance. Becky had fallen asleep holding Kawonu. Lieutenant Smith gestured for Nelly to stay with Becky and for the rest of us to follow him into a tent. There, a man sat at a desk with some papers in front of him. He made some marks on a map.

I heard Margaret ask him about our father. Certain words in English kept coming up.

The man examined his papers again. He shrugged and looked irritated as he spoke to her.

She frowned and told us, “We’ll come back in the morning.”

Raven asked Margaret, “What did he say?”

Margaret sighed. “He said he doesn’t speak Cherokee, and the names on the list don’t make sense to him. He said, ‘You’ll have to come back in the morning. All I do is mark you people off.’ But he also said that if Daddy gave them any trouble, he probably had already been marched on and whipped. And he doesn’t have any blankets for us.”

Mama and I went back to the wagon and grabbed our baskets. The chill in the air made me glad we had packed so many clothes.

Nelly woke Becky. She climbed out of the wagon, and soldiers moved the wagon away. Raven rubbed Nelly's back as we walked to find a place to camp.

Many people were asleep, but there was crying too. Some of the wailing was that of babies, but I also heard some older Cherokees crying. It sounded like a funeral.

Margaret found an empty spot where we could put our blankets down. Becky retrieved Kawonu from the basket and placed him in between us. We took off some of our layers of extra clothing.

Mama looked around the camp. "I'm going to see if anyone knows what happened to our neighbors." She kneeled down in front of Becky and said, "Don't you go off alone now. You hear?" She turned to me. "And you see she doesn't." Mama stood up and disappeared into the dark. It was hard to watch her walk away while all around us people wept.

My sisters and I squeezed together, like we always did at night.

"Ew," Becky said. "This place stinks."

I had to agree. Even though we were outside, it didn't smell like it. It smelled of chamber pots and sickness. In spite of the odor, Becky fell back to sleep quickly. I tried to stay awake waiting for Mama.

When I next opened my eyes, though, it was dawn. I felt hot and sticky. I reached out to push the quilt off me. It was tight, and I had to pull hard to get it off. I guessed because the weight of another body was holding it down.

"Scoot over, Possum," I said.

Becky didn't respond. I tugged at the blanket again to free myself and heard the rustling of her dry cornhusk doll. I sat up, expecting to see Becky and her duck in a deep sleep.

Instead, Mama was on one side of me and Margaret was on the other.

Becky and her duck were gone.

CHAPTER SIX

Fort Wool at New Echota
June 2, 1838
Early morning

"Mama!" I shouted.

Margaret and Mama sat up with a start.

"Becky's gone!" I said.

Mama looked ready to cry.

"She was here asleep just a little while ago," Margaret reassured us. "She couldn't have gone far."

"Raven, Nelly, you two stay here and wait for Becky in case she comes back," Mama said. Margaret, Mama, and I split up to look for Becky.

Mama went one direction, and I started to walk a different way. Margaret grabbed my hand. "You and

I will stay together. We don't want to look for you next."

I figured I could take care of myself, but I didn't argue. We walked around slowly, seeing the camp for the first time in daylight. People were sleeping under dirty blankets. The smoke of several cooking fires was starting to fill the air.

I heard Becky before I saw her. I stopped Margaret. "Listen," I said.

"Kawonu?" Becky's tearful voice yelled. At home, Becky's voice filled the rooms. Here in camp it was tiny.

We followed the cry to the camp's farthest corner. Becky cried and called for Kawonu. Her duck was nowhere to be seen.

"He's gone," Becky cried.

I put my arm around her.

Just then, Mama ran up.

"Kawonu is gone," Becky repeated.

"I'll bet he's flown h—" I started to say, but stopped myself. Home was lost to us. "I bet he'll be at our new home," I said instead.

Margaret and Mama gave me a look. Becky's sobs slowed.

Mama knelt down and brushed back Becky's hair. She wiped her tears. "Now listen. You can't go off by yourself. You remember what happened yesterday? You heard what that soldier said? That he wouldn't be happy until every Cherokee in Georgia was dead?"

Becky began to cry harder. Mama looked at me.

"It's not safe to go off alone here," she said to us.

The night before, Margaret had told us Cherokees were not allowed to leave the camp. However, white strangers and soldiers were free to come and go.

We returned to the others. Raven had started a campfire. Nelly was stretched out on the blankets, eyes closed. Becky curled up next to her, exhausted from crying.

Mama and Margaret went back to the tent where we had checked in with the unhelpful soldier the night before. We hoped they could find out if Daddy had been captured. Surely if he had escaped the soldiers, he would eventually come here to look for us.

Raven asked me to watch over Nelly and Becky. While we had been looking for Becky, he had received word that his sister Charlotte had just been brought in.

Even though it wasn't the ideal situation, I was happy to hear that I would see my best friend again. "Can you bring Jenny back with you?"

Raven shook his head. "Jenny and Steven ran off when the soldiers came. The soldiers wouldn't let Charlotte go into the woods to get them or wait for them. And her husband was out hunting. No one knows where he is or if he even knows they are here."

Raven was gone before I could ask him anything else. I was frightened. Jenny's little brother, Steven, was the same age as Becky. I couldn't imagine having to take care of Becky in the woods by myself.

Becky murmured, "I hope they don't get eaten by bears."

It didn't make me feel any better.

Margaret and Mama returned shortly.

"The soldiers made a list of all the animals our people brought in with them. Then they took them away. Our horses are on the list," Margaret said. "We think they took Daddy on to Ross's Landing in Tennessee with some of the men they thought would be trouble."

I thought of my Grandpa running back into the cabin, and I remembered the story Daddy had told us about the Georgians wanting to whip Cherokees. I hoped they hadn't whipped my daddy. Or worse.

"Daddy and Raven paid a hundred dollars apiece for those horses," I said.

"They took good care of them too," Becky added.

"They sure did," Mama said, smiling. She used to say Daddy loved that horse more than he loved her. "I have to go get our rations."

"It seems strange to stand in line for food," I told Becky after Mama left.

"Why didn't they let us bring what we had?" Becky said.

"I don't know how you can think about food. This place smells terrible," I said.

"Of course it does," Becky said. "The latrine's right there." Becky gestured toward a line of people on their way to the bathroom.

Margaret decided to search for a clean spot. While she was gone, Raven and Charlotte arrived. We were all happy to see Charlotte, but she looked tired and discouraged.

Margaret soon found a new spot for us, with

enough room for our family and Charlotte's, whenever they arrived.

We settled in, but Charlotte couldn't sit still. She watched the people walking around the camp, hoping to see her family or someone who might know where they were.

"I sent word to a neighbor," she told us. "A white woman who I hope will go look for Jenny

and Steven. My husband was off hunting when the soldiers came. I have no idea where he is either."

I felt afraid for them, but I knew better than to say so. I nodded in sympathy.

"I feel completely lost without my family," Charlotte said, starting to cry.

Becky and I hugged her. We couldn't help crying a little bit too.

That night, we boiled our dinner over a fire in the small pot Mama had brought. Other people had no way to cook their ration of salt pork. We were also glad Mama had grabbed the flint pieces we needed to start a fire. Other families had to light their wood off of our fire.

As soon as it got dark, I went to bed. It was hard to sleep. So many people made for a noisy campground. In the dark, there always seemed to be crying.

I woke several times. In the woods, an owl hooted. It sent shivers down my spine. I heard another noise and turned over. I wondered if an animal was getting into our supplies.

I started to sit up, but then I froze. My eyes had adjusted enough to the darkness to see two large figures. They were standing over our baskets. I heard the plink of a violin's string.

I sat up and screamed.

CHAPTER SEVEN

Fort Wool at New Echota
June 2, 1838
Late night

My family and several other Cherokees woke up. Raven and some other adults surrounded the two white men.

"They were taking our things," I said.

"Liar," one man hissed at me. I didn't speak much English, but I understood that.

A soldier came over to see what was going on. He stepped in between the men and us. Margaret told the guard what had happened.

One of the white men scowled at her and said something. He handed the fiddle to the soldier.

Someone asked Margaret what the thief had said. Margaret translated, "He said they were just going to borrow it."

I heard several adults laugh.

"Y'all go back to sleep," the soldier said. He held his bayoneted musket between himself and us. Swiftly, he escorted the two white men away.

We rearranged our campsite and moved our baskets so they were in the middle of where we slept. It was hard to get comfortable. Becky had been awakened by the disturbance too. I put my arms around her. "Goodnight, Possum," I whispered.

"Goodnight, Mary," she whispered back.

I listened as people began to breathe softly as they fell asleep. I hated how much the men had frightened me. Underneath the snores and sleepy breathing, I heard Becky crying.

"What's wrong, Becky?" I whispered.

"I don't want to say," she sniffed.

"Everything's all right, Possum. Those men left."

At this, she cried a little harder. I waited until she calmed down. "Becky?" I said quietly.

"Do you think they took Kawonu?" she stuttered.

I had to think fast. "That duck wouldn't have let those men grab him without a fight."

I leaned close to her ear and quacked quietly. Becky giggled. I quacked again. From somewhere in the dark, someone shushed us. We fell asleep giggling and quacking as quietly as we could.

June 3, 1838

Jenny and Steven were still missing the next morning.

A white woman came into camp and walked from family to family, looking for things to buy cheap. I recognized her. Her name was Mrs. Scales.

I ran to her. "Do you know where Jenny Goingsnake lives?" I asked.

The woman thought a minute. “The Goingsnakes lived up by me. Why?”

“She and her brother hid in the woods. The soldiers won’t let their mother go find them. Would you look for them?” I asked.

The woman nodded. “That’s kind of a lot of trouble for me. How would you be able to pay me?”

I thought of the only thing I had that my family didn’t need. “I’ll be right back,” I said.

I emptied my small burden basket and ran back to Mrs. Scales. In exchange for it, she agreed to try to find Jenny and Steven. I said I would hold onto it until she came back with them. Mrs. Scales frowned again, but left the camp immediately.

I hoped she would find them soon. No Cherokee could remain in Georgia much longer. Soon we would all be moving closer to Ross’s Landing in Tennessee. It would be the first of many water crossings on the trail. Some people were organized to leave with the soldiers almost as soon as they got to camp. Raven didn't want to leave until his niece and nephew were found. Neither did I.

The day continued to pass, hot and slow. We were going to be separated into detachments, groups of about a thousand Cherokees that would depart for the west at different times. There was a rumor that we would stop going west soon. It was too hot, and the drought was making it hard to move hundreds of people together.

A new shipment of rations arrived. Mama and I went to get in line. As we stood there, those who had gotten their rations walked by, looking unhappy. A friend of Mama's stopped to talk to her.

"Look," Mama's friend said. She opened the bag of cornmeal. Tiny yellow worms with brown heads wiggled in the grain.

Mama shook her head. "Better cook it extra good," she said.

Her friend laughed and retied her bag. The line moved slow, and I thought about all the bags filled with bugs when each person walked by.

When we returned to our campsite, Mama had me start mixing up the buggy meal for dinner. I missed having Kawonu to feed bugs to.

I crouched on the ground next to our cookfire. I turned my head when I heard some excited voices coming from the direction of the fort's entrance. Mrs. Scales was walking in with Jenny and Steven in tow.

"Jenny!" I shouted with joy.

I ran to her and hugged her tight. She was dirty and tired. Hers and Steven's faces and arms were scratched, and their clothes were torn.

Charlotte ran up and wrapped them both in her arms. Raven smiled for the first time in days.

"I'm glad you didn't get eaten by a bear," said Becky.

"Me too!" said Jenny.

I grabbed my basket and gave it to Mrs. Scales. She disappeared quickly.

That night, we ate dinner with Jenny's family. In the morning we would all leave for another prison camp near a place called Vann's Plantation. It would be closer to Ross's Landing, where the boats were supposed to be that would take us west. Walking there, we would share a wagon with at least one other family besides Charlotte's. All of our supplies would be loaded in the wagon. Only people who couldn't walk would be allowed to ride.

"I don't mind walking," Nelly said as we ate. "Riding in a wagon makes me feel all shook up."

I was glad Nelly felt good enough to walk. Still, I thought if I could get away with riding instead of walking now and then, I might prefer it. Raven frowned, though. I wondered if he thought about the horses that had been taken from him and Daddy. The soldier in charge of the camp had auctioned off all the livestock Cherokees had brought to the camp. Raven's and Daddy's horses sold for twelve dollars each.

That night, Jenny, Becky, and I huddled close under the stars. Jenny told us about hiding in the woods and gathering food. Mrs. Scales had found Jenny and her brother when they had started a fire to cook a fish.

"I sure am glad to be back with my family," Jenny said, before she fell asleep.

A few minutes later Becky whispered to me, "I hope we catch up to Daddy."

I whispered back, "Me too."

Internment Camp, Near Vann's Plantation
June 30, 1838

"There are no more Cherokees in Georgia," Margaret said one morning.

Cherokees in Tennessee, Alabama, and North Carolina had all been rounded up too.

Vann's Plantation was one of ten prison camps in Tennessee. People were being separated into smaller groups called *detachments*. The first three of these detachments had been escorted by federal troops and had traveled by water. We had yet to be assigned to a detachment.

That evening, a man named Will came into the camp. He had risked his life to escape the first detachment. We sat down around a fire at another family's camp and listened to what he had to say.

"I believe the survivors of the first detachment are already in the western Cherokee Nation," he said.

Becky and I looked at each other.

"The soldiers who were escorting us were cruel." He looked around. "I came back here because there is no place else for a Cherokee to go," he went on. Many had died, he explained, including enslaved Africans.

"There is no food or water, and many drowned falling from the overcrowded boats," he explained.

Becky grabbed my hand. I looked over at Mama, but she was staring at the campfire.

"The soldiers took babies from their mothers and put them in wagons with the sick and the dead," Will said. "They said the children were slowing them down." He shook his head. Tears trickled down his cheeks. "Chief John Ross has heard about it and is trying to get the government to let the Cherokees organize the rest of the removal."

No one said anything.

"For now, that's the best we can hope for," Will said.

I spoke up. "Is my daddy with them?"

Will turned and looked at me. He nodded. "Your daddy was still there when I took off," he said.

My heart fluttered a bit, happy to hear news of Daddy.

It was getting late, so Becky and I got up and walked back to our site.

"I hope Daddy is safe," Becky whispered to me.

"I bet he's already building us a home," I said, trying to put Becky's mind at ease.

"Really?" Becky exclaimed.

I nodded, wanting to believe it more than I did.

July 2, 1838

As a result of the drought and the disastrous first three detachments, the trips west came to a standstill. Everyone agreed we should remain during the sick season. In the summer, the bad air caused an illness called *ague*. It gave us chills, headaches, and fevers.

Finally, Assistant Chief George Lowery came to tell us what was going to happen next.

He stood on a stump and spoke loudly. "The river has dried up too much for the boats. There is no water for drinking, either. Traveling overland in the heat is going to be hard on everyone, especially the very young and old. We are going to stay in the camps until September first."

As weeks then months passed, camp conditions grew worse. There was not enough shelter when it rained, and the sun beat down on us most days. We slept on the ground outside with little clothing.

Sickness visited everyone. Some people had cramps and diarrhea. The flu spread through camp too. The only doctor at the camp had turned out to be a dentist.

One night in August, I couldn't sleep from stomach pain. I tossed and turned. Becky and I both went to the bathroom in the night, sick to our stomachs.

When we settled back in, Becky whispered to me. "My mouth is dry."

I felt too sick to get her water. All I could do was say, "I'm sorry, Becky."

Margaret heard us talking and brought us water.

I shook my head, though. I knew I couldn't handle anything in my stomach. I wondered if this was how I was going to die.

In the morning, I felt a bit stronger, but Becky couldn't get up. Jenny watched us with a frightened look. Then she disappeared. Mama made us some hot tea with dried leaves she had packed. I drank some. Becky turned her head away at first.

"I wish Grandma was here to take care of us," Becky groaned.

Margaret called it the "bloody flux" and said it was spreading through the camp. People were dying from it. Wails of mourning haunted the camp. Mama stayed close to Becky. She pressed a cool cloth to Becky's forehead.

"Mama," I whispered, "is Becky going to be okay?"

I almost cried when Mama didn't answer me.

CHAPTER EIGHT

Internment Camp, Near Vann's Plantation
August 10, 1838

In the morning, I heard Mama crying softly.

"Mama?" I sat up.

Mama rocked Becky gently in her arms.

"It's okay," Mama said. "Her fever broke." Mama wiped her tears away quickly. She didn't want anyone to hear her. "She needs to rest, though."

Jenny brought some cornhusks and string and sat next to me and Becky. She and I each made a doll. When Jenny finally got Becky to smile, everyone felt better.

That night, Jenny, Becky, and I slept near each

other. I held Becky close. I wished I could keep her healthy and safe.

September 1, 1838

The drought continued. Boats still could not take us downriver. An overland crossing of thousands of people would require plenty of water for drinking and for the oxen and horses too. Removal to the west was still on hold.

The camp's population had grown to more than nine hundred, including a large group of Creeks who had lived among the Cherokees. We all dreaded another day in the dirty camp.

"I'm hungry," Becky complained. Jenny and I exchanged looks.

I got an idea. I found Margaret and suggested we gather medicine for the next leg of the trip.

She disappeared and asked Lieutenant Smith if

we could forage outside the camp. He agreed, but made Margaret promise that none of us would run off. As small a kindness as it was, not every soldier would have allowed us to leave camp.

Becky and Steven were excited.

"We can hang the plants to dry on the lean-tos," Becky said.

"Maybe we can trap a rabbit," Steven added.

We got some other children together. They were nearly dancing with joy to leave the camp. But when we walked outside the camp, my heart fell. Everything was so brown.

"The drought?" Jenny asked.

Margaret nodded.

The younger kids didn't seem to notice. They chased grasshoppers and looked for rabbit tracks.

"Look," Becky squealed.

Becky had spotted a buckeye tree.

The fruit of the buckeye looks like a hairy pear.

The little kids ran through the woods looking for another tree. Margaret, Jenny, and I watched them.

"It's almost like home," Jenny said.

"Almost," I said.

We each gathered several buckeyes.

"Make sure you leave some to grow into new trees," Margaret said.

We walked out of the woods and pretended we had never been taken from our homes a little longer.

Lieutenant Smith met us at the camp's entrance.

"What'd you find?" he asked Margaret.

Margaret explained how buckeyes can be ground up and dried. When dropped into pools of water, the ground-up buckeyes stun fish.

"Remember how fun it was to fish with these?" Jenny said.

We gave a handful to Lieutenant Smith. Margaret explained how to grind them up and dry them.

"Fish would be better than salt pork," said Becky.

I nodded.

For a little while it had felt almost like a normal day.

October 18, 1838

The cold weather brought the rain we had needed since June. One older couple was brought into camp without blankets. The elderly pair stood in the rain, looking pitiful. Raven went out from under our lean-to and nailed together wood scraps to provide them with shelter from the rain.

My family huddled under our wooden lean-to. Scattered around the camp were at least seventy similar structures. Rain didn't fall directly onto our heads, but there was no way to stay out of the mud that pooled around us. Nelly tried to make herself as small as possible. Her baby was due soon.

While the rain came down heavily, Becky cried. She had been kneeling to keep her bottom out of the mud, but her legs gave out. She splashed down, splattering everyone.

I was miserable too. Even Margaret and Nelly, who usually managed to lift everyone's spirits, didn't have the energy to comfort Becky. I reached out and pulled her back up.

"Possum," I said, my teeth chattering. "Do you remember the song 'Orphan Child'?"

Becky nodded.

I hoped I remembered the words. I started to sing about the orphan child crying and listening to the creator, "u we do li s di ka ne gv ga tv gi a tsi sa."

Margaret joined me on the next line. Together we sang, "u ni do da na. nu ne hv na u na da ni ya dv," asking the father to not abandon the child.

Nelly joined in as we repeated the first verse. "u we do li s di ka ne gv ga tv gi a tsi sa."

The rain let up a little. Becky began to sing too. "u ni do da na. nu ne hv na u na da ni ya dv."

Around our family, other voices rose too. It felt like the entire camp was singing. "u we do li s di ka ne gv ga tv gi a tsi sa. u ni do da na. nu ne hv na u na da ni ya dv."

As we sang the song, the rain stopped.

I crawled out from the lean-to and pulled Becky out with me. "There's always going to be rain, Possum," I said. "Sometimes you just have to sing while you're all wet."

October 20, 1838

Almost five months after we had been forced from our home, my family loaded what we had into a wagon to walk to Chattanooga, Tennessee. We would camp there until it was time to depart for Ross's Landing, our first major water crossing. After Ross's Landing, there would still be a good distance to travel before we reached our new home. It felt like the journey would never end.

Our group would be lead by Richard Taylor. Mr. Taylor was a Cherokee warrior and leader. He had been to Washington many times to plead our case. When it looked like we would have to leave Georgia, he had sent his own family west but stayed behind to help the rest of our tribe. He was going to lead nearly a thousand of us to our new home.

For every fifteen people, one ox-drawn cart was assigned. Only those who were unable to walk because of sickness or age could sit in a wagon. That morning, the camp was in chaos. Not wanting to waste time, some people had already started walking after packing their belongings in a wagon. Charlotte, Steven, and Jenny had packed up and gone on ahead.

Nelly wasn't much help and was moving slowly. She looked as if her whole body hurt.

"What's wrong, Nelly?" I asked.

Nelly gritted her teeth. "I think I'm sick," she said. Then she doubled over and fell to the ground.

CHAPTER NINE

Internment Camp, Near Vann's Plantation
October 20, 1838

Mama was quickly at Nelly's side. "You girls stay here," she ordered me and Becky. She and Raven helped Nelly stand up and began to guide her back toward the camp. Margaret followed right behind them.

Some of the wagons began to move.

"Mama!" Becky wept. "We have to go get Mama," she said, trying to pull away from me. I threw my arms around her and held her with all my might.

"Mama told us to stay here," I cried.

Becky was starting to wail. I was having trouble holding on to her skinny arms.

Suddenly Margaret walked up and wrapped Becky in a hug. "We start the walk to our new home today."

"Where is Mama?" Becky asked.

"She's with Nelly," Margaret said.

"Where's Nelly?" Becky demanded.

Margaret sighed. "Nelly's going to have her baby today."

Becky's mouth dropped open.

"Mama doesn't want the rest of us to stay here any longer," Margaret said. "She, Nelly, Raven, and their baby are going to come in a day or two."

Becky cried. Margaret lifted her into the wagon. The man who was going to drive our wagon walked up and asked if it was ready to go. Margaret begged him to wait another few minutes.

Margaret reached into our burden basket

and pulled out a small blue and white blanket. She leaned down and handed it to me. Margaret whispered to me, "Mama is afraid of all the sickness here. She doesn't want us here any longer." Death seemed to be happening daily. Every day the camp grew filthier. The rains and cold had made it worse.

Margaret stood up and reached into the basket again. This time she pulled out a larger woven blanket with similar blue stripes and colors. She handed this blanket to me too.

"Take this to the infirmary. Hurry now," she said. "Nelly will need these."

I ran to the makeshift hospital tent. I found Mama and Nelly standing outside. Mama rubbed Nelly's back and leaned over, whispering to her.

I ran up to my sister. "Nelly, Margaret told me to bring you this."

Nelly smiled. Her face was flushed and sweaty. Her lips tightened for a moment, then she took the white and blue striped cloth from me. "Wado, Mary." She thanked me with a light hug.

Mama turned to me. "Watch over your little sister," she said. "She's never been away from me."

I wanted to point out that I had never been away from Mama either. I stopped, though. Instead I said, "I love you, Mama."

"I love you too. Always stay together, the three of you. Now go on."

I turned away from Mama before my tears began. I wanted to be done with crying. I didn't want Becky to see my tears. The night before, I couldn't wait to leave this camp of sickness and death. Now I wept to leave Nelly, Raven, and Mama behind.

Camp in Chattanooga, Tennessee
November 1, 1838

It had been eleven days since we had seen Mama, Nelly, and Raven.

Cherokees arrived from all over at Ross's Landing. The new camp was even more crowded than the one we had left. New people came and went all the time, but there was no word or sign from Mama.

As we were loading up to go once more, good news came for Jenny's family. Her father was alive. He was helping organize Mr. Hildebrand's detachment. They would be the last detachment to depart, meaning they would leave after our group. I was happy for Jenny's family, but sad for myself.

Jenny, Steven, and Charlotte quickly removed their items from the wagon. They would be staying at Ross's Landing another week. I barely had time to hug Jenny before our group had to leave the camp.

"Well," I said, "see you soon."

"Yes. We're all going to the same place." She

walked with me a short distance, then turned and ran back to her family.

Our wagons were going to be taken across the Tennessee River by ferry. Other flat-bottom boats were taking people across the water.

That made me nervous. In the camp, I had heard stories that many Indians, both Cherokee and Creek, had died when forced onto overcrowded boats. The passage between the shores was at least four miles. The boats would spend the day going back and forth, transporting wagons and people across the river. Our detachment would end up being spread out over miles.

Each time we got closer to the front of the line of people waiting to get on a boat, Margaret would stop us and let others go ahead. I noticed she kept looking toward the back of the line. Finally, I realized Margaret was hoping Mama would catch up with us.

“I’ll just go to the back and see if they’re there,” I whispered.

“No!” Margaret reached out to grab me, but I was already running. I followed the line of people as it snaked across the road. A flash of white and blue in a woman’s arms caught my eye. Nelly was standing next to a wagon. Next to her were Mama and Raven.

“Mama!” I cried, waving. I turned to go get my sisters. I hadn’t known how important it was for my family to be together until we had been torn apart.

Margaret was angry with me for running off but forgot about it the minute she saw Nelly’s new baby. He was eleven days old. She called him Tsali. He was tiny, but strong. His black hair was thick and dark. The thick fluff matched his dark eyes. I wondered how soon babies could smile. I, for one, finally had something to smile about.

The Banks of the Piney River
Missouri
March 8, 1839

Weeks passed, then months. After leaving Kentucky, we walked and were ferried through a small portion of Illinois and then a larger portion of Missouri. In early March, it snowed so much we had to stop traveling. It wasn't like the weeks we were snowbound back in January, but we began to wonder if winter would ever end. We also had days of rain where the tents wouldn't keep us dry.

But that one day in March was beautiful. I hoped spring was coming. Becky was excited. She talked about the things she loved about spring as we walked.

"Not wearing shoes!" was among the things she celebrated. Becky slipped off the plain muddy moccasins she wore. How light they had been when we first started our walk west. How dark they had gotten. Becky shook the dried mud off her shoes.

We had repaired our everyday moccasins several times on this walk with new soles. Mama kept our beaded pucker toe moccasins tucked away.

Our wagon stopped for a few minutes so we could enjoy the sun. Nelly laid Tsali out on his blue blanket. He napped. The trail seemed less awful on that beautiful afternoon.

As it got closer to evening, the wind turned cold. We were not in a place where we could camp yet, and a light rain began. I put on all the clothes I had. I held Becky close, trying to keep her dry and warm. We both shook with chill. My toes hurt from the wet.

Nelly fell behind, carrying Tsali. We slowed down to walk with her. In her arms, Tsali was wrapped tight. Raven stood on one side of her and Margaret on the other to try to protect her and the baby from the weather. By the time we came to a place where over eight hundred of us could camp for the night, poor Tsali's nose ran and his lips shook blue with cold.

We tried to get a fire going. The wind whipped, blowing out the tiny flames. We ate leftover cornbread and huddled together, trying to warm up. In the night, snow began to fall. I wondered if we would ever be warm again.

Arkansas
March 16, 1839

The smell of salt pork woke me. I was hungry but sick of the smell of that pork. For months we'd eaten nothing but salted meat and ground corn. I wished Daddy was here and that he could go hunting. But even if he was with us, hunting would be difficult. Back in Georgia, the soldiers had taken all our rifles.

I wondered if we went to the woods, would there be mushrooms like we used to gather? I stood up, trying not to wake Becky or Margaret. Beneath their closed eyes were dark circles. Their faces were thinner than the summer before.

I looked around for the rest of my family. Raven was gone too, but Nelly was curled around her sweet baby boy. He had run a fever for almost a week. The day before, he had been too exhausted from sickness to cry. Since we'd left Georgia, at least ten babies had been born. I tried not to think about how many of those babies had already passed.

Mama stood near the fire, holding her skirt back.

"Where's Raven?" I asked.

Mama looked worried. "A white man came up the road there and started talking to him. He spoke Cherokee. I guess he worked for the Old Settlers. Raven followed him into the woods."

The Old Settlers were Cherokees who had come west before the forced removal. Some came before the Treaty of New Echota. They had built a life and homes here. They had been forced to leave Arkansas for the west, just as we had to leave Georgia.

I worried, wondering why Raven had followed the man. Foolishness was out of character for him.

Other people in the camp began to wake up and prepare for the day's journey. Suddenly we heard the sound of a single rifle shot.

Everyone looked toward the woods.

No, not Raven! I screamed in my head, thinking of my grandpa. We were so close to the end of our journey.

CHAPTER TEN

Arkansas
March 16, 1839

Nelly came running out of the tent, carrying Tsali. Becky and Margaret followed quickly behind.

"Where's Raven?" Nelly cried.

Mama gestured toward the woods, but none of us spoke.

Nelly quickly handed Tsali to me. I noticed his body was warmer than it should have been. Nelly went to where Mama was making breakfast and picked up an iron skillet. Mama reached out and grabbed it from her.

"Nelly, that skillet won't be any good against a

rifle," she said. "You stay here with your baby. I'll go see what happened."

Mama ran toward the woods, and Margaret followed.

They stopped when they heard tree branches snapping, as if something large was moving toward them.

Raven stepped out of the woods. "Yona!" he called out, holding up the rifle. He had shot a bear, and we would have a feast.

Everyone around us moved with a life I thought we had lost. Gadugi made the work easier and ensured there was enough for the families around us. Some people made cornbread. Other children and I gathered greens and mushrooms in the woods. Margaret and Raven passed out the bear meat, while Mama cooked our portion over the campfire. It was a nice break from salt pork.

Nelly sat holding Tsali, but she didn't eat.

Raven sat down next to her. He put some bear meat between pieces of cornbread and whispered into her ear.

"If Tsali won't eat," she said quietly, "I'm not going to, either."

All day she hadn't been able to get Tsali to eat. She held him close to feed him. He turned his fevered head away. His lips were dry. His little body was too warm.

Finally, Mama went to her. She fed Nelly like a child.

That night, we wore all the clothes we had. The fires didn't provide much warmth in the dark. If you slept too close to the fire you could burn. Too far away, and the cold licked your bones.

As I was about to doze off, I heard Nelly begin to cry. *Nelly must be scared,* I thought, feeling sad for her. The cold and rain was too hard on a baby. I thought about how some of the children left behind on the trail had been as young as Tsali. So many promises of the future died with each child. Mamas died along the trail and left behind orphans. Many elders also died, and their knowledge died with them.

The next day, Tsali continued to weaken. His eyes looked without seeing. Nelly tried to place milk in his mouth since he wouldn't nurse. He wasn't interested.

Two days later, Tsali died.

"We're going to go," Raven told Mama.

Nelly stood holding her dead son. He was wrapped in the beautiful cloth she had woven when she was happy. "We're going to find a place for burial," said Raven.

"Wait a moment," Mama said. She went to the wagon and pulled out a cloth. Grandpa's violin was wrapped inside of it. She handed it to Raven. "You can trade or sell it."

Raven nodded. He promised they would rejoin us soon. Nelly seemed barely there when she hugged us.

George Woodhall's Farm
March 24, 1839

Our detachment finally arrived at George Woodhall's farm. It was one of the places the U.S. government had chosen for the Cherokees to rest and pick up food and supplies during the first year of our rebuilding. Other detachments had already stopped here. Tents would be needed until we could build our new homes, and we would need food until we could plant and harvest crops. Margaret and Mama set about hammering the stakes into the ground for our tent. We had no interest in sleeping in the open one more time.

"You girls go ask people if they have seen your daddy," Mama said.

All around the farm, I saw people I remembered from home. "Have you seen my daddy?" I asked. Everyone shook their head no.

Please don't be dead, I begged. *Please be waiting for us.*

We walked until we reached the road. A new group was coming in. Becky and I searched for our daddy's face in the crowd. At the back, several people were on horseback. One of them was wrapped in a blue and white striped blanket. A man with his long hair in a braid wrapped in red cord led the horse with a short rope.

"Nelly!" I shouted. "Raven!"

Nelly looked over and smiled sadly at Becky and me. Raven helped her down. Becky and I crowded her. It had only been five days since we had parted, but on the trail parting was often forever.

Raven invited Becky to ride the horse to the stable.

"Yes!" Becky squealed.

Nelly reached down and took my hand. "Show me where you have the tent set up."

I led Nelly through the camp. Mama would be so happy to see her. I thought of all the places where my family had cried on the trip to the new Cherokee Nation. Over the last ten months, we had wept over cruelty, sickness, and death. We had cried for the people and places left behind, the land where our people's story had begun.

Everyone had lost something. Some had lost everything. I thought of my grandparents. I thought of Daddy and Becky's pet, Kawonu. I thought about Tsali, whom Nelly missed with all her heart. We had started walking with more than a thousand other Cherokees, and we'd lost more than fifty from our detachment alone.

I was glad to be done walking, but I wondered if I would ever be happy again.

Nelly and I approached our tent. It stood clean and new, ready to protect us from the spring rains. As we approached, a thin, dark-haired man stepped out of the tent. I froze. Tears stabbed at the corners of my eyes.

"Daddy," I whispered.

I ran and jumped into Daddy's arms. Mama stepped out of the tent too. She ran to Nelly and took her in her arms.

I noticed Margaret was repacking our things.

I heard Becky holler, "Daddy!" moments before I felt the impact of her wrapping her arms around our Daddy's legs. He set me down and picked up Becky.

"Well," Daddy said, "do you girls want to spend the night here on this farm or see the cabin?" He grinned at Mama.

"Home!" Becky squealed.

I hugged Daddy hard. For the first time ever, I felt like crying because I was happy.

A NOTE FROM THE AUTHOR

The taking of Indigenous land, including the Trail of Tears, was one of this country's darker chapters. The organized theft of Cherokee land in the southeast found its horrific conclusion in a poorly planned imprisonment and a torturous march. The events in this book took place over the course of ten months. Many Cherokees spent much of this time in prison camps. There were deadly consequences.

This continent was once populated entirely by Indigenous people. Five hundred years later, after European colonization, we are less than two percent of the population of the United States. The term *Trail of Tears* also refers to the removal of other Southeastern tribes (the Choctaw, Chickasaw, Seminole, and Creek) that began prior to Cherokee removal. Meanwhile Indian removal was happening all over the country, often violently.

Before forced removal, the Cherokee population is believed to have numbered around 17,000. The Trail of Tears, a walk of about 1,000 miles, resulted in the death of approximately 4,000 people, or 24 percent of the population. An untold number of enslaved Africans and intermarried white people died on the route as well.

The government took several steps to evict the Cherokees. The state of Georgia passed laws that discriminated against Cherokees. The federal government violated treaties and laws in support of Georgia. In 1805, President Thomas Jefferson said he wanted to remove our Indigenous ancestors. This was part of the philosophy that made Andrew Jackson popular with Americans. He was elected president in 1828. Finally, in 1838, under President Martin Van Buren, the Cherokees were removed.

Fewer than one hundred Cherokees, a group that came to be known as the Treaty Party, signed the illegal Treaty of New Echota. The treaty gave up Cherokee land in Georgia in exchange for money and land west of Arkansas Territory. The document promised the Cherokees would leave within two years. The treaty was strongly opposed by the Ross Party. More than 15,000 Cherokees signed a petition against the treaty. Some white Americans also opposed the removal of Indigenous people, including poet Ralph Waldo Emerson and politician and settler Davy Crockett. The Cherokees took their case to the Supreme

Court and won, but President Jackson ignored the ruling and prepared for removal. He ordered roads, forts, and prison camps to be built on Cherokee land. Men were enlisted in troops and instructed to remove the Cherokees.

I am a citizen of the Cherokee Nation of Oklahoma. Growing up in the former Indian Territory, I thought I understood the Trail of Tears. I researched and read books by Choctaw citizen Tim Tingle, who wrote on the removal of his people. I did a lot of other reading. However, I didn't want to write this story until I had visited our Cherokee homeland. My daughters and I traveled to New Echota. As we walked around the site, I realized how much I hadn't understood.

The Trail of Tears was not just a terrible forced march. It was the loss of the places where our stories were born and where our ancestors were buried. It was a loss of elders who carried knowledge about plants, arts, and language—some of which cannot be recovered. It was also the needless deaths of Cherokee mothers, fathers, brothers, and sisters. The Cherokees became refugees, driven from their homeland on a continent that rightfully belonged to Native peoples and their nations.

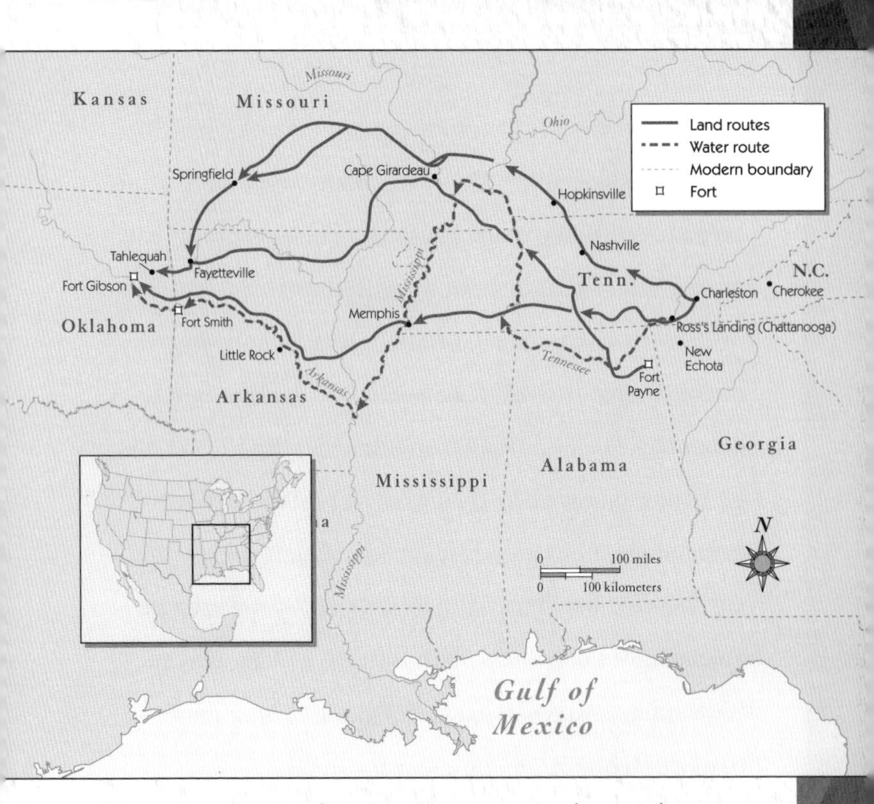

Forced removals of Native Americans in the southeastern United States followed both land and water routes.

When I began writing for children, this was exactly the kind of story I wanted to tell. That is not to say it was fun or easy. It was difficult and traumatic. These are my people. I would not be here if my ancestors had not survived this stage of genocide. My daughters would not exist, and I can't think of anything more sad. I felt a responsibility to tell the story as accurately as I could.

Mary's story is historical fiction. However, the hardships she and her family faced are based on real-life events. I consulted many historic documents during my research, including interviews with survivors of the Trail of Tears in *The Indian-Pioneer Papers* at the University of Oklahoma; *Cherokee Removal: The Journal of Rev. Daniel S. Butrick*, a Baptist missionary who had worked with the Cherokees in Tennessee and followed them to Oklahoma; a visit to New Echota maintained by the Georgia State Park system; a report by the state of Tennessee's Division of Archaeology; and a report by the National Park Service and Georgia on the Cherokee Removal, *Forts Along the Georgia Trail of Tears*.

Employees at all these sites, as well as employees at the Cherokee Nation of Oklahoma, the Cherokee Heritage Center, and Cherokee genealogist Twila Barnes, were generous with their time and knowledge in answering my questions. Keetoowah Knight answered many Cherokee language questions. Indigenous writers Ruby Hansen Murray (Osage), Traci Sorell (Cherokee), and Art Coulson (Cherokee) read an early draft of this book. My husband, Heath Henry, who is a history teacher, shared his Trail of Tears time line with me. In order to write about slavery, I read a community-sourced document by P. Gabrielle Foreman, et al., "Writing About Slavery/Teaching About Slavery: This Might Help." My daughters, Elena, Ana, and Angie, were helpful and supportive.

I hope you choose to learn more about Indigenous people. Research should always start with the tribe as your primary resource. We are the experts on ourselves.

Though what happened to the Cherokees was wrong, we survive. We are still here. Our capitol in Tahlequah, Oklahoma, has stood for more than 150 years. Wherever our people are is home. Today there are more than 355,000 enrolled Cherokee Nation of Oklahoma citizens living all around the world. Two other federally recognized tribes can trace their ancestors to the Cherokees impacted by the Trail of Tears—the United Keetoowah Band, also of Oklahoma, and the Eastern Band of Cherokee Indians in North Carolina. I hope that Mary's story encourages you to think more deeply about history. Our ancestors were people, not numbers.

GLOSSARY

ague (EY-gyoo)—malaria or some other illness involving shivering or fever

bandolier bag (ban-duh-LEER BAG)—a large, heavily beaded pouch with a wide strap

bayonet (BAY-uh-net)—a long blade that can be fastened to the end of a rifle

burden basket (BUR-duhn BAS-kit)—a Cherokee burden basket is a tall basket with a round top and square bottom, often tied to a person's shoulders with a strip of cloth like a backpack

creator (kree-AY-ter)—used as a name for God, or an all-powerful being

detachment (dih-TACH-muhnt)—a party of people separated from a larger group

elder (EL-dur)—an old person, especially one who is respected or is an authority

forage (FOR-ij)—to go in search of food or medicine

internment (in-TURN-muhnt)—the state of being kept as a prisoner, especially for political or military reasons

latrine (luh-TREEN)—an outdoor toilet that is usually a hole in the ground

lean-to (LEEN-too)—a rough shelter with a sloped roof

lieutenant (loo-TEN-uhnt)—an officer of low rank in the armed forces

makeshift (MAKE-shift)—made from things that are available to use for a short time

moccasin (MAH-kuh-sin)—a flat, soft leather shoe or slipper

musket (MUHS-kit)—a type of long gun that was used by soldiers before the rifle was invented

plantation (plan-TAY-shuhn)—a large area of land where crops are grown

ration (RASH-uhn)—a limited amount or share, especially of food

smokehouse (SMOHK-hous)—a building where meat or fish is smoked

stockade (stah-KADE)—a fence made of strong posts to protect against attacks or keep people inside

syllabary (SIL-uh-ber-ee)—a set of written symbols used to write a given language

wado (wa-DOH)—the Cherokee word for "thank you"

yona (YO-nah)—the Cherokee word for "bear"

MAKING CONNECTIONS

1. Why do you think the removal of the Cherokees is called the Trail of Tears? Cite an example from the text that supports your answer.

2. Choose a character from the book who changes. What is this character like at the end of the book versus the beginning? Write a paragraph about this change using evidence from the text.

3. Mary was forced to leave her homeland, unable to take much with her. However, the Cherokee Nation of Oklahoma has now existed for almost 200 years. It is "home" to many Cherokees. Write a letter describing what home means to you.

ABOUT THE AUTHOR

Andrea L. Rogers is a citizen of the Cherokee Nation of Oklahoma and a graduate of the Institute for American Indian Arts. At IAIA, she got her MFA and was mentored by several strong Indigenous writers and teachers. She teaches art at an all-girls public school and is the mom of three daughters. She is at work on a novel and a short story collection. In the summers, she teaches basket weaving at a Native American summer camp. She grew up in Tulsa, Oklahoma, and currently lives in Fort Worth, Texas, where she serves on the board for the Fort Worth Public Library.